The Dollhouse Caper

The Dollhouse Caper

BY JEAN S. O'CONNELL

with illustrations by Erik Blegvad

A Harper Trophy Book
Harper & Row, Publishers

Library of Congress Cataloging in Publication Data
O'Connell, Jean S.
    The dollhouse caper.

    Summary: Worried that the growing Human children will soon
discard them, the Dollhouse family try to think of a way to save
themselves and their home.
    [1. Dolls—Fiction] I. Blegvad, Erik, ill.   II. Title.
PZ8.9.035Do   [Fic]   75-25501
ISBN 0-690-01042-7

"A Harper Trophy Book"
ISBN 0-06-440236-3 (pbk.)

Published in hardcover by Thomas Y. Crowell, New York.
First Harper Trophy edition, 1988.

Contents

The Dollhouse Caper

The Bang-y Beginning

The long sleep was over once again. The father lifted the dollhouse from the high shelf, tipped it backward so all of its tiny furniture and people slid and crashed into the walls.

"Here it comes!" he yelled, and he lowered the house to the mother.

Mrs. Dollhouse, lying under the living-room couch, stared at the father's huge fingers curling through the window. Moving day was always so rough!

Sometimes Mr. Dollhouse's head fell off. Besides that, Mrs. Dollhouse often couldn't even *find* Mr. Dollhouse or the children until night-time because, once waked up, the dollhouse people couldn't move around by themselves until the human people had gone to bed.

A long time ago girl Dollhouse (whose real name was Ruth) had asked why this was so; she didn't like being still all day. And Mrs. Dollhouse had told her that was just a Fact of Life, like the long, long sleep from early spring, when the dollhouse was put onto a high shelf and covered, rather like a birdcage, with a dark cloth, until it was brought down again at the beginning of the Christmas season.

"Pooh," Ruth had said, tossing her head because Mrs. Dollhouse was trying to comb her hair which was made of some terrible kind of nylon and nothing could be done with it, "that means we are controlled by the humans completely, and I am going to jump out and roll myself under the radiator and they will never find me."

"We are *not* completely controlled," Mrs. Dollhouse said very firmly, pulling at a tangle. "We do exactly as we please all night. Anyway, if you lived under the radiator you'd get dusty."

"But it's not fair!" Ruth said. "We only *come* to life in the *night*time!"

"It's fair," Mrs. Dollhouse said, tying a ribbon around Ruth's head. "The humans only come to life in the *day*time."

"Oh," Ruth said, "I never thought of that!" and off she went to play with the piano, quite happy.

Ruth was still happy now, many years later. She always celebrated the first night down from the shelf by shouting, "Hurray! the controls are off!" and she would lift the lid of the music box piano and then lead her brother and the baby on a wild marching dance through all the rooms of the dollhouse to the tune of "Here We Go Round the Mulberry Bush," which was the song the piano played.

Usually Mrs. Dollhouse was as happy as the children on moving night. But this year, she worried. Ruth, she knew, would be as happy as ever—after all, Ruth never grew up. But Mrs. Dollhouse knew that human children did. And human children owned the dollhouse.

Besides that, they were boys.

There were good things and bad things about the boys growing up, and Mrs. Dollhouse counted them as she slid from under the couch

to under the piano. First of all, maybe they would be calmer—so maybe they would *not* stuff Mr. Dollhouse into the toilet head-down this year, but allow him to sit on the sofa instead. That would be a Good Thing. But they might decide the dollhouse was "babyish"— and put it back on the shelf forever. That would be a Bad Thing.

But the very worst thing of all would be that the humans might give the dollhouse away, now that the boys were so big. No matter how hard they tried, the Dollhouses had never found out anything about the history of their house except that it had been bought, empty of people or furniture, in a secondhand store long ago by Mrs. Human. And sometimes, in the long bright daytimes when she couldn't sleep, Mrs. Dollhouse worried about this more than anything.

Now the house was carried, father-fashion, with furniture and people dropping out of the windows, down to the playroom, where it was set on an old trunk near the window.

The mother followed the father, picking up things that had dropped. But, mother-fashion, she just dumped them all into the dollhouse in a pile, with Ruth on top of the cradle which was on top of the painting that hung over the fireplace. "I'll fix it up later," she said. "It's time for lunch," and she went into the kitchen.

The father stood still for a few minutes, looking at the messy house as the boys came in from the yard where they had been playing soccer. One of them gave the ball a last kick through the doorway, and the soccer ball whizzed

across the playroom and crashed into the dollhouse, rocking it backward and then forward again. Everything fell out on the floor.

The father turned around. "There are not very many rules in this house," he said in a huge voice, "but ONE of them is that we play soccer out of doors." And he knelt on the floor and began to pick up the dollhouse people and furniture.

"I'm sorry," the three boys' voices said all together. Mrs. Dollhouse noticed with a shudder that one of the voices was very deep this year.

"Nice to see it back again," the middle boy said, and he replaced the toilet in the bathroom and stuffed Mr. Dollhouse into it, head-down.

"It looks kind of beat-up," the youngest boy said as he put Ruth on top of the piano, standing on her head.

Then Mrs. Dollhouse heard the eldest boy's new deep voice. "Aren't we getting a little *old* for this?" he asked.

No one answered him. "After all," he said, "a *doll*house in a house that's full of great big boys." He picked up the chimney and put it on top of the roof where it belonged. "Really," he added, "it's embarrassing."

Spooks?

That deep voice, that threat, kept Mrs. Dollhouse awake all day even though she was so tired from moving. Would the eldest boy argue the others into putting the dollhouse away on the shelf, not to be brought down again for years and years?

The Dollhouses slept when they were put on the high shelf each spring because it was as if they all had batteries that could only be charged by the children. None of them had real batteries, of course, but, out of sight, out of mind on the shelf, the toys lost their pep, and just became objects. It was not painful, but it was sad. It was called, "Waiting For The Next Generation."

Worse, would the eldest boy argue the others into getting rid of the dollhouse entirely, by giving it away?

All day no one cleaned the little house or hooked up the electricity. Usually the three boys set to work immediately, arranging things after their mother dusted each piece of tiny furniture. But this year the dollhouse sat un-touched. In fact, the humans all went out to something called a square dance, didn't come home again until late—and went right to bed.

But night came at last, and the first thing Mrs. Dollhouse did was to pull her husband out of the toilet bowl and set his head on straight. I'll save the worrying until later, Mrs. Doll-house thought as she admired her handsome husband, dressed as usual in a tuxedo.

Mr. Dollhouse brushed off his trousers, kissed Mrs. Dollhouse good evening, and went off with her, hand in hand, to find the children.

It was not easy. They had to climb over a

toy chest and a typewriter just to get out of the bathroom.

"Lucky the stairs are nailed in," Mr. Dollhouse said. "In the mess those humans have left this place today, we'd have to hang and drop to get downstairs at all."

Mrs. Dollhouse patted him on the arm. He was often out of sorts when he first woke up, especially if he had spent the day in the toilet.

Even as they went down the elegant curving staircase together, they could hear the music box piano playing, and then Ruth came dancing into the hallway. Behind her was Todd, her brother. They were having such a fine time dancing and marching that they barely kissed their parents hello as they jumped through the rooms.

"Todd, where is your arm?" Mrs. Dollhouse asked, for the sleeve of Todd's little green and white checked shirt hung empty, and Todd was slightly off balance as he danced about.

"It's around somewhere," Todd said. "Don't worry, Mom."

"We certainly *will* worry," Mr. Dollhouse

said. "It's the one with that nice wristwatch painted on it."

"Okay okay," Todd said. "I know it's not *very* lost."

Then they all marched around singing, "The controls are off!" Sure enough, they found Todd's arm in the china closet, and he actually stood still long enough to have it attached again. Then he could help shoving furniture and lifting things as they all looked for Baby.

But Baby was nowhere to be found. They searched the cradle and the crib, the closets. In the kitchen they looked everywhere.

"Glurg!" said a voice from inside the washing machine.

Mr. Dollhouse opened it, and there was Baby, neatly wedged in.

Pulling did no good. Only Baby's nightgown slipped off.

"Stop, stop!" said Mrs. Dollhouse, "you'll hurt Baby's beautiful head." Baby's head was made of china, wonderfully shaped, with gentle coloring on the round pink face.

Todd looked around. "Aha!" he said suddenly, and lifted an enormous object from the shelf in the kitchen. "At last we've found a use for Great Spoon."

The spoon was one of the thousands of gifts the humans had given to the dollhouse family. Usually it hung on a tiny nail against the kitchen wall. It was handsome, but, compared to the Dollhouses, as big as a shovel, so they named it Great Spoon, and never used it.

Together Mr. Dollhouse and Todd managed to get the spoon into the washing machine, rather like a shoehorn, and pried Baby loose. He shot across the kitchen floor like an olive out of a bottle.

"Glurg!" Baby said triumphantly as he was

picked up and hugged lovingly by everyone in the family. Mrs. Dollhouse put Baby's nightgown on him again, sat him in his high chair, and set about making a little breakfast.

It was hard to do in the dark. "I do wish," Mr. Dollhouse said as he arranged things in the kitchen, "that one of the humans had remembered to plug in the electric cord."

"I think it's romantic," Ruth said, "eating by only the light of the Outside."

What she meant was the light from the street lamp outside the humans' house, which shone through the huge bowed window where the dollhouse was placed.

"It's a great light for playing robber," Todd said, and he slipped into the black shadow cast by the kitchen door, leaped out yelling, "Your money or your life!" and scared his father half to death. He was told to sit down NOW and behave himself.

The baby thought all this was very funny, and he chortled and laughed and waved his fat little arms about so charmingly that pretty soon everyone was laughing and everything was funny. It was funny that Mrs. Dollhouse had to have Todd help her lift the frying pan onto the stove because it was half again as big as she was.

"We could put the pan on the floor and use Great Spoon as a shovel and just have a picnic and not even *use* the table," Ruth said, and they all rocked back and forth with laughter.

"And afterward we could use Great Spoon as a bat and slam loose all those cans the humans glued to the kitchen shelves," Todd added.

"Oh, the problems of dollhouses!" Mr. Dollhouse said, wiping his eyes because he was laughing so hard. "Wouldn't you think that when the humans glued the cans in to keep them from falling out—never thinking, by the way, that we can't eat what's in them—that they would have put a little glue on that red chair? Remember how I used to sit down every single night at breakfast and fall under the table because Mrs. Human always propped the leg?"

"And you always forgot," Mrs. Dollhouse said, smiling. "My, I'm glad *that* chair got lost." She laughed a little. "When I *think* of the number of times you children fell overboard the first year trying to get from the nursery to the bathroom—"

"That was before we learned how to get the door open," Todd said. "Sometimes, just for fun now, I get to the bathroom from the nursery the old way, creeping around the edge."

"You really should use the door," his mother said, serious for a moment.

"But you have to know just how to pull it," Ruth said. "It's always stuck, and then it makes a terrible screechy noise."

"Remember the year the human boys made the stairs into a ramp?" Mrs. Dollhouse asked. "And we all had such fun sliding down and had to boost each other up?"

They laughed because it was funny and they laughed because it was good to be together again as they ate by the light of the Outside.

Suddenly, with a tinkling crash, the street light went dark.

In the inky blackness that followed, the Dollhouses all heard a noise behind the humans' house. A tiptoeing, sneaky noise.

Together Ruth and Todd and their mother and father rushed to the windows to look out toward the street.

And there, looking in, was a FACE.

The Dollhouses froze. The face was peering around the edge of the dollhouse to see into the playroom and the hallway and the dining room beyond.

Another face appeared, a younger face.

"Too dark," the older face said. "Can't see much. Gotta flashlight?"

17

The beam shone right through the dollhouse windows.

"Not bad," the older face said. "A TV, some silver junk—"

But the younger face was looking at the still dollhouse family. "All those little fellas are staring at me," he said. "Like real—"

"A big help *you* are," the older one said. "Come *on,* flash that light into the other room—"

A thump sounded from upstairs in the humans' house.

"Douse da light," the older face said. "Let's split." And the two men ran off, out of the yard, down the street. The Dollhouses could hear, from a distance, the noise of a car starting up and driving off.

"What do you make of *that?*" Mr. Dollhouse said.

Kevin Has Plans

"Waah," yelled Baby. But, just as Mrs. Doll-house was picking him up, and he was half in and half out of his high chair, a human came creeping down the stairs in his bare feet, walk-ing very carefully so as not to make any noise.

The Dollhouses stayed put; there was noth-ing else to do.

It was the eldest boy, Kevin, and he bumped into a rocking chair as he came into the room. "Ow!" Kevin jumped about for a little, holding his injured foot. "Now why," he said in a whis-per to himself, "is it so dark in here?" He went toward the dollhouse and looked out of the big window. "No street light," he muttered. "That's funny. Some jerk must have smashed it. Guess that's what woke me up. Lucky thing, or I would have slept all night."

He knelt down on the floor in front of the dollhouse.

Mrs. Dollhouse stared at this boy, at his great bare feet sticking out of his pajama pants, his huge hands, his tousled hair, still blond and curly, that she remembered so well from the very first time she had seen him, when he was five. It was astonishing, this human business of growing.

"I have Plans for you," Kevin said, and Mrs. Dollhouse's heart jumped for joy. He still talks to us, she thought happily. Maybe he didn't mean what he said, about being embarrassed.

"Yes, Plans," Kevin said again, and he reached into his pajama pocket and pulled out three round balls with long heavy strings sticking out of them. "These are real cherry bombs," he whispered into the dollhouse, "and if Dad ever found out I had them, he'd have a fit." He

reached into the house and pushed carefully
against the wall under the stairway until it came
loose. "In they go!" he muttered, "into the
secret place," and he slipped the three red balls
into the space under the stairs and then fitted
the piece of wall back into place.

"Playing with the dollhouse?" a voice said
suddenly. It was the youngest boy speaking.
He had come downstairs so quietly that no one
had heard him, not even Mrs. Dollhouse.

Kevin jumped. "You have to sneak around
like that at night?"

"I got hungry," the youngest human said.
His name was Harry. "I had a dream about a
peanut-butter sandwich." He knelt down on
the floor next to Kevin, took the baby out of

Mrs. Dollhouse's arms and put him back into the high chair. Then he took all of the family and sat them down at the kitchen table, all but Mr. Dollhouse. He put Mr. Dollhouse in the living room, playing the piano.

Harry lifted the tiny piano top and propped it up with the little stick inside. The underside of the top was a painting of tiny ladies and gentlemen dancing around a tree. "I think this piano is the most beautiful thing in the world," Harry said. He sighed. Then he began to arrange all the furniture. "Here," he said to Kevin, "you make the beds."

Kevin took the pile of little patchwork quilts in his hand and just knelt there, watching Harry so busy fixing up the house. "No, thanks," Kevin said, and put the quilts in a pile in the bedroom. "I'm too old for the dopey dollhouse."

"Then why were you kneeling here?" Harry asked, hanging Great Spoon up where it belonged.

"I was just looking at what happened to the street light." Kevin pointed out of the window.

"Wow!" Harry said, and became so interested in the street light that he never remembered to ask Kevin why he had come downstairs to see it when he could just as well have seen it from his bedroom window.

"If you plugged in the lights, those dollhouse people could see a lot better," a voice said from the hall, and the middle brother came into the playroom. "Is this the way we're doing it this year?" he whispered, "playing dollhouse in the middle of the night?"

"Oh, Peter," Kevin said. "Don't be silly. I think we're too big for the dollhouse, so there."

"Speak for yourself," the middle boy said.

"Mom *said,*" Harry said, and his voice began to tremble.

Kevin stood up. "Come on, Harry, I'll get you a sandwich. I *know* Mom said."

The middle boy, Peter, stood in the playroom, scratching his head. He had bright red hair and it itched a lot. He could also think better when he scratched his head.

He went toward the dollhouse, looked over it at the broken street lamp outside, whistled softly to himself, then stooped and plugged in the electric cord to the dollhouse. In the glare of the tiny bulbs, Peter looked carefully at each room. Finally, under a pile of furniture, he found a framed picture about as big as a postage stamp. He looked at it for a long long time. Inside the fancy golden frame was a painting of mountains and a waterfall. Very gently, Peter hung the picture over the fireplace in the living room.

Then he picked up Mr. Dollhouse and stuffed him, head-down, into the toilet, and joined his brothers in the kitchen for a snack.

It did not, of course, take very long for the boys' mother to come downstairs, ask them all *what* they were doing up in the middle of the night making such a racket, and shoo them all back to bed again.

As he went upstairs, the middle boy, Peter, turned and rushed quickly down to the dollhouse. He took Mr. Dollhouse out of the toilet, set his head on straight, and sat him down in the living room where he could see the beautiful picture of the mountains and the waterfall.

His mother saw him and smiled. "Don't forget to switch off the lights," she said.

Peter clicked the switch on the edge of the dollhouse wall.

"Why, the street light's broken!" his mother said. "I wonder how *that* happened. Well, I'll call the town about it in the morning."

"It always takes a month before the town gets around to fixing it," Peter said cheerfully. "Boy, it sure makes it dark around the outside of our house, doesn't it?" and he scampered off, up to his room.

"It surely does make it dark," the mother said, half aloud. She turned to go upstairs, and a small hand slipped into hers.

"It's not going to go, is it, Mom?"

The mother looked down and smoothed her youngest son's hair where it stood up in a little fountain.

"Someday, Harry, even *you*'ll outgrow it. . . ."

"I wish everything would stay the same FOREVER," Harry said. "Like in the dollhouse."

They stood next to each other, looking sad.

"Would you like me to carry you upstairs piggyback?" the mother said at last.

Harry turned and ran ahead of her. "No thanks, Mom," he said. "I'm too big for that now."

Let Todd Handle It

In the dollhouse, as soon as the humans had left the room, Mr. Dollhouse switched on the lights, and everyone gathered in the kitchen again to try to finish their breakfasts.

"Boy!" Todd said, "are those humans dumb! All standing around saying, 'My, my, the street light's out,' and then going back to bed again. First thing *they* know, those two awful men are going to come in and rob this place."

"You're scaring your sister," Mrs. Dollhouse said, putting her arm around Ruth, who was beginning to tremble.

"It's how they start," Todd went right on. "It's called casing the joint. I'm *sorry* if it's scary, Ruth. But it's true!"

"Casing the joint?" Mrs. Dollhouse asked. "Where did you ever learn anything like that?"

"One night when the humans forgot to turn off the television set," Todd said. "It ran all night and I watched it. It had these bad men on it and they all robbed people and first they came and looked secretly to find out where things were and they called the looking Casing the Joint."

"I don't remember that," Mr. Dollhouse said, sitting up very straight.

"How could you?" Todd said rudely. "You had your head in the toilet."

The baby laughed and banged his spoon on his high chair for joy.

But Mr. Dollhouse looked unhappy. "Now I remember," he said. "Your mother and Ruth worked all night trying to get me out, I was so jammed in. And they kept calling for you but you never answered, and all that time you were sitting around watching television. That's *not* very loyal." He stood up. "I have heard the human father say often enough that television is a waste of time and I must say I agree with him!"

Todd finished his eggs in silence, not looking up from his plate. At last he said, staring at his milk glass, "I was only trying to help. But I guess, if you don't want to know . . ."

There was no answer. Todd looked around the table, at his father who was red in the face and at Ruth, who was trembling; at the baby, who was putting egg on top of his head, and

at his mother, whose permanent frown was even deeper than usual. "Probably," Todd said, "they'll come in because those humans don't even suspect anything is wrong, and they'll take all the silver and the television set and wow, maybe they'll even take us!"

Ruth and the baby started to cry. Todd sprang to his feet. "Think of how that'll be!" he shouted. "The whole house. And we'll end up in some thieves' secret place and one day the police will storm in, and we'll be the only people who know the secret and we'll tell them everything and be heroes!"

He leaped up on the table, brandishing his fork.

Ruth screamed, the baby fell forward in his high chair, Mrs. Dollhouse put her head down over the table, and Mr. Dollhouse stood up, his hand in the air.

"That's impossible," he said. "You can't even move when humans are around. Now get down off the table and let's try to be logical."

So Todd, very pleased that his father had at last listened to him, climbed down into his seat again and everyone was quiet.

"First of all," Mr. Dollhouse said, "do we all think Todd is right?"

"Yes!" everyone shouted, and Todd stood up and bowed.

Mr. Dollhouse reached over and pushed on Todd's head until he sat down again. "Second of all," he said, "we all *want* to warn the humans. Right?"

"Oh, yes! Yes!" Mrs. Dollhouse said.

But hers was the only voice.

What Next?

Mr. Dollhouse looked at Ruth and Todd and the baby in a very surprised way. "Well?"

"Glurg!" said Baby, pointing to the washing machine.

"He hated being stuffed in there all year," Ruth said, patting the place on Baby's head that had no egg on it. "And I don't especially like standing on my head on the piano either."

"They stay up so late sometimes," Todd said. "And they keep dismembering me. They keep growing and their hands are so big. That's why. I don't think they *mean* to take my arm off or my leg, but they do it in their clumsy way."

"They have been very good to us, Todd, over the years," Mr. Dollhouse said. "You're forgetting the toy trains and the typewriter and the soft rugs and the special cowboy hat and—"

"And you're forgetting that you spend an awful lot of time in the toilet, Father," Todd said.

Mrs. Dollhouse rapped Great Spoon against the wall for silence and got it. "You're *all* forgetting everything important!" she said. Her voice was not quite steady because she was so close to tears and had been trying all evening to keep her worries about the growing-upness of the human boys to herself. But she was a mother, and she took a deep breath, wiped the corners of her eyes with the dish towel, and said, "Since we're being so logical, first of all, have you all forgotten the toy-shop shelf?"

She looked around the table. Ruth and Todd and Baby were trying not to meet her eyes.

"Remember that year, all of us wrapped in cellophane? Why, when Mrs. Human bought us and carried us here, we were so delighted

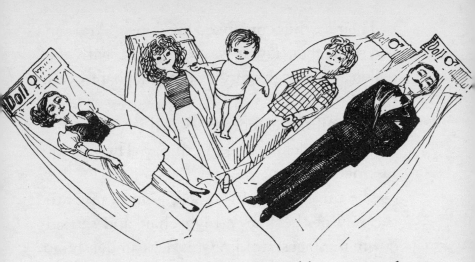

we didn't mind *any*thing. An old, unpainted dollhouse with no rugs, no electricity—not even any beds—"

Ruth and Todd stole glances at each other. They were remembering how it had been in the empty dollhouse at first. They used to run around at night, sliding through the doorways and playing "camp-out" in the dining room.

Ruth said, in a small voice, "The first piece of furniture was the piano. Remember those great make-believe concerts we gave, Todd?"

Todd nodded. "Baby would crawl along the keys, and I'd get inside and close the top over me and yowl and scare everyone to pieces."

Their mother continued speaking. "And can you remember how it was *before* that, with you children all wriggling inside the cellophane every night?"

They all remembered, silently.

"And there are the kind things. The cat, for instance."

The cat, hearing his name, jumped up onto the tray of the baby's high chair and settled down in stages, folding his legs under him, curling his tail about his body so that just the tip flicked for the baby to play with.

"The middle boy—Peter—he did the kind favor for the cat, as I remember," Mr. Dollhouse said.

"That's right." Todd nodded. "It was the middle one, Peter. I remember how he looked and looked at the cat always being attached to its bowl, drinking, and then once, when everyone was out, Peter just snapped the cat's nose loose from the dish—and freed him forever!"

The cat purred and licked himself.

"Too bad he left that piece of the cat's nose

on the dish," Ruth said, "where it didn't break off perfectly."

The cat hissed at her.

"All the same it's boring that Mrs. Human always glues the cat back in place when she thinks of it," Ruth added, shrinking back a little from the cat's fangs.

"Lucky the glue she uses is weak," Todd said, "so Peter can always snap him loose again."

Suddenly Mr. Dollhouse said, "And the electric lights. I have always been so fond of the electric lights. Peter's the one who worried about them and made his father put the switch right *on* the house, where we can reach it, as I remember."

"And it was Peter who sawed off the handle of the frying pan when he saw it wouldn't fit crosswise in the kitchen," Mrs. Dollhouse said.

"He's going to be an artist; I heard him say so," Ruth added.

They were quiet for a few moments.

Then Mrs. Dollhouse asked, "And have you all forgotten about the Christmas tree?"

That was fundamental. Now the whole family sat, each thinking his or her own thoughts. The Christmas tree went back to the beginning, back to the nights when the dollhouse first began, when it was hidden in a closet, and worked on by Mrs. Human whenever she could steal a few minutes away from the boys. The eldest boy, Kevin, had asked for a dollhouse for Christmas, and every member of the dollhouse family remembered that glorious morning when they emerged from the closet, in their newly painted house, to be set on a low table next to the humans' Christmas tree.

Kevin was five years old that year, and he just sat down on the floor in front of the dollhouse and looked. He looked at the family, all seated around their new dining-room table, at the kitchen with the interesting blocklike sink and stove, at the nursery, where there were two beds and a crib, all with miniature patchwork quilts. He noticed that there was a telephone in the hallway and that the toilet was made of real porcelain. He did not reach out to touch anything.

Finally the human mother said, "Do you like your dollhouse?"

"It has no Christmas tree," Kevin announced.

And all the Dollhouses loved him immediately.

Much of Christmas day was spent making a Christmas tree. Kevin, who could still use his imagination better than his hands, ran outside in the snow in his pajamas and tore off a bit of spruce tree near the house. Then he found his modeling clay and stuck the twig of spruce in it so it would stand upright. He took bits of Christmas wrapping paper and poked holes in them with a pencil and put them on the branches.

The next younger brother, Peter, who was only two, watched him admiringly. "No star," he commented.

Kevin grabbed at Harry, who was unable to move because he was only four months old then, and deftly removed from the baby's nightgown a loose gripper—and a small piece of nightgown, but the hole didn't show much.

He stuck this on top of the tree for a star. And
then he put the Christmas tree in the living
room of the dollhouse.

The Dollhouses thought it was beautiful—
they had never seen a Christmas tree before.
And every year the eldest boy made a new one,
each time more skillfully, and decorated it with
silver and red balls made of aluminum foil,
which he hung from the branches on threads,
and little Indian glass bead chains.

But no matter how elegant the new trees

were, the Dollhouses always longed for the old tree with the gripper on the top.

"That was Harry's gripper, wasn't it?" Ruth asked dreamily. "Good old Harry, he's an understanding soul. . . ."

Mr. and Mrs. Dollhouse looked at each other, smiling. They both remembered when the boys had once converted the dollhouse into a combination garage and gas station and had zoomed little cars through the doorways and put a toy gas pump, of all things, right in the middle of the dollhouse living room. A bit of wood over the stairway was called a car ramp, and the human boys were forever saying "Fill 'er up!" and making little binging noises as they pretended to pump gallons into the cars.

Every night Mr. and Mrs. Dollhouse spent valuable time dismantling everything so they could lead a more or less normal life while the humans slept—if you can call it normal to have a gas pump in the living room.

Eventually Mr. Dollhouse took to pushing the gas pump overboard each night.

For three days the boys argued, blaming each

other for the misplaced gas pump. Finally the older two decided that the smallest one did it. After that, every morning little Harry came padding downstairs in his red, footed pajamas. He would pick up the gas pump from wherever it had fallen and replace it in the dollhouse living room. Then he always patted the house on its bright red roof, and padded softly back upstairs to bed again.

He never told the others he did this.

"If he weren't so grotesquely large," Mr. Dollhouse said fondly one dawn as the baby boy toddled down the stairs, "he'd be adorable."

Mrs. Dollhouse looked around at her family, all quiet. "What do you think now?" she asked. "Ruth, you first—"

"Now I think about it, it would be awful to let the humans be all robbed and case-jointed and everything," Ruth said. She added wistfully, "Maybe their growing-upness will make them stop putting me on the piano on my head. . . ."

"Baby?" Mrs. Dollhouse asked.

"Glurg," said Baby, and he climbed out of his high chair, squishing the cat on the way, crawled over to the washing machine and began to climb in.

"I guess we know how *he* feels," Mr. Dollhouse said, laughing.

"Todd?"

Solemnly, Todd said, "What I guess it all comes down to is—is—this is home. That's all there is to it. However," he added, "before you all get mushy about this, if we go to the trouble of warning them, what'll they do for us?"

And the words rushed out before Mrs. Dollhouse could stop them. "Maybe they won't put us up on the shelf to Wait For The Next Generation—"

"That's a threat?" Todd asked.

Mrs. Dollhouse sighed. "It's a—possibility — now."

"Oh dear," Ruth said.

"Waah," said Baby.

"Yuk,"said Todd.

Looking at their sad faces, Mrs. Dollhouse

just didn't have the heart to say anything about being given away.

Mr. Dollhouse stood up again, leaned his hands on the table, and looked very serious. "Let's *act*," he said. "Starting right now. We can't talk to them, we can't move when they're around. What shall we do?"

The Giant Blood Spot

They all thought for a few minutes. Even the baby crawled back across the floor to Mr. Dollhouse, who picked him up and sat with him in his lap. Putting his dimpled elbows on the table, Baby rested his face in his chubby little hands and tried to think too.

The cat stalked off the tray of the high chair and settled himself importantly among the dishes on the table. His long tail flicked as he tried to find a way to curve it about himself without getting egg on it, but the tip of it went into a water glass, and twitched out so quickly that the glass tipped over and water ran across the table and into Todd's lap.

With great interest, not moving from his place, the cat watched Todd leap up, grab for a napkin, and manage to knock the glass onto the floor, where it broke.

Then Todd and his father had to get the broom (a wondrous object that Mrs. Human had made out of straws and a swizzle stick, which stood outside the front door) and clean up the mess. It was difficult to do because of the great height of the broom—two dollhouse people were needed to push it. Ruth found the dustpan, and, once they had all managed to sweep the glass fragments into the pan and were wondering what to do with them, Todd said:

"I know! Let's try warning everyone through Harry! Let's break a window!"

"What good would that do?" Mrs. Dollhouse asked. "Really, Todd, you are so violent."

"Well," Todd said, "you know how it is with Harry—I mean, he's closest to us in spirit, don't you think?"

Everyone nodded.

"Like in the gas-pump thing. He always seems to understand about us. Agreed?"

They agreed.

"If we break one of our windows, old Harry's going to notice. If we break a window on the street-light side of the dollhouse especially. Like old Harry's going to see that broken window and look up and be reminded of that broken street light and Harry's going to go running to his mother and say, 'Hey, Mom, I think the dollhouse people are trying to tell us something.' Something like that."

It seemed suddenly a brilliant idea, and Todd cheerily took Great Spoon off its hook and flung it back over his shoulder. But just as he was about to swing it Ruth said, "No, no, Todd! It has to be broken from the outside IN!"

Todd lowered the spoon from his shoulder and stared at her.

"Don't you see?" Ruth said excitedly, "if you break it from the inside out, all the glass is going to fall down into that crack between the wall and the trunk thing our house is on, and they might not notice it for months."

"Years," Mrs. Dollhouse said. "I have never known any of the humans to clean behind the trunk. I looked over the edge once and the gap was full of huge cloudy things and old pencils and pieces of the Monopoly set. . . . Ruth's right, Todd."

"But there's no *way* of knocking out the window *in*ward," Todd said. "No place to balance on that side of the house. Anyone who tried it would fall into the gap and be lost forever." And he shuddered at the thought.

Mr. Dollhouse stood up and took off his tuxedo. "I'll do it," he said. "But you'll all have to help. Now what I'll do is lean out of the kitchen door—and if you'll all hang on to me I can have both arms free. Then I'll swing Great Spoon sideways and smash this window"— he pointed to the one nearest the table—"and the glass will go all over the kitchen!"

He hoisted Great Spoon onto his shoulder and went to the doorway. Todd held him around the waist. Mrs. Dollhouse held Todd around his waist. Ruth hung on to Todd, and Baby, on his uncertain feet, hugged Ruth's knees.

"When I say 'Hang on!' you all pull backward while I lean out and whack the window."

They all took deep breaths and got ready.

The cat put its head down and went to sleep on the table.

"Hang on!" Mr. Dollhouse yelled. He leaned forward over the terrible gap and swung the spoon.

Mrs. Dollhouse and Ruth and Todd and the baby held tight.

Crash! The window broke inward, all over the kitchen table and the cat, which at last hopped away.

"Pull me back!" Mr. Dollhouse ordered.

They pulled. For one sickening moment, Mr. Dollhouse teetered over the gap, then, boom, they all fell over backward with Mr. Dollhouse safely on top of the heap.

Mrs. Dollhouse helped him into his tuxedo again, and Ruth and Todd picked up the baby, who had been on the bottom of the heap but his head was undamaged.

Across the sky a streak of sunlight broke the clouds.

"That was a good night's work," Mr. Dollhouse said, swelling out his chest a little. "Good day, everyone," and he went off to resume his place looking at the beautiful picture in the living room. All the others returned to the places they had been put by the humans earlier in the evening.

No sooner was this done than Harry came pad-padding down the stairs. He always rose at dawn, even as he had when he was only a little fellow. Only now, instead of the footed pajamas, he wore red furry slippers and striped flannel pajamas and a brown bathrobe that had belonged to his brothers before him.

There were things Harry liked to do in the morning. For instance he liked to stroke the leaves of the African violet plant because they were soft. His mother always told him it would damage the plant to touch the leaves, so Harry did it before anyone was up to stop him. He liked peanut butter for breakfast and that made his father nervous so he always ate an enormous peanut-butter sandwich and a Coke shortly after arising. Harry also set the clock on the mantel in the playroom because it always stopped at four in the morning and he liked to reach around behind it to start the pendulum moving again. What he liked most of all was that his mother and father often said to guests, when asked, "Yes, the clock is very old but Harry takes care of it and you know, it has run perfectly for years and years now, never stopping."

This dawn Harry, clutching his battered bathrobe about him, stood in the playroom looking at the clock, eating his peanut-butter sandwich and shivering because the Coke was so cold. Oddly enough, the clock had not stopped last night, so he had no excuse to reach into its ancient insides, but it reminded him of the mantel clock in the dollhouse so he went to look for it and found it upstairs in the dollhouse nursery.

Lovingly, Harry placed the clock on the living-room mantel, underneath the painting. Then he reached into the dollhouse and propped up the top of the piano, and sighed. There were the tiny ladies and gentlemen, dancing so beautifully, and the little music box played "Mulberry Bush" ever so faintly in the early morning.

Harry sat on the floor in front of the doll-house and sucked at the top of his empty Coke bottle. And this made him think of the miniature Coke bottles that were always in the icebox in the dollhouse kitchen.

Of course he saw the broken glass right away. And he saw that Great Spoon was lying on the floor and he had a distinct memory of hanging it up before he had gone to bed. Harry looked at the little kitchen window, all jagged, and at the splinters of glass on the floor of the kitchen and thought that that was the most mysterious thing he had ever seen.

Immediately, he checked on all the doll-house people—they were all where they belonged. Nothing else was disturbed.

Stooping down, Harry sighted out, through the broken dollhouse window, through the big bowed window of his own house, right into the broken street lamp, which he could see clearly now that the sun had come up.

"Wild," said Harry to himself. "Well, they'll all blame it on me, so I'll just clean it up, and if I take all the jagged glass out of the window

frame, maybe no one will notice that there's
no window there at all."

He used a damp paper towel to pick up the
glass fragments. Then he took the jagged glass
out of the tiny window frame—and cut his
hand. Not badly. Only one drop of blood. It
covered the whole kitchen floor in front of the
icebox and looked very impressive.

Mrs. Human found Harry trying to put a
Band-aid on his hand when she came downstairs to cook breakfast. She became so inter-

ested in undoing the adhesive, which had stuck to itself, that she forgot all about asking Harry how he had cut his hand so early in the morning.

It was a school day, and the boys rushed off to school, and Mr. Human rushed off to work, and Mrs. Human rushed about tidying up her own house, just wiping at the roof of the dollhouse with a dustcloth as she went by, and then she rushed off to go shopping.

And Harry, when he came home from school, gave just one quick look into the dollhouse, and a quick listen to his brothers and was happy that no one had noticed that the window was missing. I'll mention it some other time, he thought.

Meanwhile, Harry rather enjoyed having a Band-aid on his hand.

A Blank Wall!

"What a flop!" Todd said that night. "Little old Harry has a persecution complex."

"What's that?" Ruth asked. She was practicing a tap dance on top of the piano.

"He's afraid the others are going to blame things on him," Todd said. "You really ought to look at the television set, Ruth, when it's on in the evening. The things you'd learn!"

"I always have to watch it upside down," Ruth snapped.

"Well, the hearing part's not upside down," Todd said. "You could *listen*."

"And learn all those scary things you've learned?"

"You want to be a dummy forever?"

"You're mean, Todd. Leave me alone."

Mrs. Dollhouse came into the living room. "Come and eat your breakfast now," she said, "and stop bickering. I've cleaned up that giant blood spot that Harry left."

So they forgot their quarrel and came into the clean shining kitchen and tried to be cheery during breakfast because they were cheery children at heart. But none of their attempts did any good. Mr. and Mrs. Dollhouse were feeling very gloomy.

"If Harry didn't get the message, who will?" Mr. Dollhouse said mournfully, pouring himself a cup of coffee.

"I wish we could talk to them. Or even write them something."

"Or draw something," Mr. Dollhouse said.

"Draw—that's it!" Ruth said. "We can try warning the middle one, Peter, with a drawing."

"Silly, we can't draw anything the humans see," Todd said.

"Silly yourself, we don't have to. Peter loves that painting, the one over the fireplace. He looks at it every single day. Sometimes he even takes it out of the house and just stares at it."

"So?"

"So, we hide it!"

"So big deal," Todd said. "That's a dumb idea."

"Let her finish, please," Mr. Dollhouse said sharply to Todd. "Many ideas seem dumb until they're explained. I should think you would have learned that on television, son."

And Todd blushed and was still.

"Well," Ruth said, "we hide the painting very very well. So Peter can't find it. And then he thinks, 'Stolen!' and he will poke around and find the empty window place, and he'll remember the broken street light and he'll go to his father and say, 'That's funny, the painting in the dollhouse has been stolen, really stolen, and I think something funny's going on,' and then his father will investigate and call the police or something. . . ."

There was silence after she spoke.

"I guess it *is* pretty dumb," Ruth said at last.

"Nope," Todd said. "It's just that we have to think some more. We could drop it down Great Gap."

"He'd never look there," Mrs. Dollhouse said, shuddering.

"Yes he would," Todd said. "The way Peter feels about that painting, he'd look under the floorboards."

"And if he finds it, how would he ever know it had been stolen?" Mr. Dollhouse asked. "Stolen things have to look that way. As if they'd been hidden."

"Let's wrap it up," Ruth said, "in a quilt or something, and tie it all up and heave it over into the gap. THEN when Peter finally finds it, he'll surely understand."

They set to work at once, using the little patchwork quilt from the master bedroom. Mr. Dollhouse climbed up and took the painting down. Working together, the family managed to wrap the quilt around the painting, and to tie it with some yarn from the handmade rug in the nursery, which had been unraveling for years.

Then they dragged the package to the kitchen door, and pushed it down into the gap. It landed with a soft thud, so they knew it hadn't broken.

Nothing happened until the following afternoon. Peter came home from school, pink-cheeked from the cold and from running up the hill. He threw his books on the floor of

the front hall, his coat on top of them, ran upstairs, said hello to his mother, went to the bathroom, came downstairs and went into the kitchen for three glasses of chocolate milk and a handful of cookies.

After that, Peter played the piano in the living room for a long, long time. He was the only boy who came home from school on time on this particular afternoon; and he sang a very long song as he played the piano, a song all his own. In the afternoon sunlight, he stretched after his singing, and went into the playroom, where he stood in the center of the room, scratching his head and staring absentmindedly at the dollhouse.

Suddenly he went close to it and knelt down on the floor. He looked at the dollhouse father, sitting in the dollhouse living room and contemplating—a blank wall.

Peter scratched his head again and began to search. He lifted up every single piece of furniture in the whole house, but found no painting. Then he looked on the floor of the playroom. He examined the couch by tearing its pillows out and throwing them on the floor. He looked under the rug, in the bookcases.

Finally he wailed a loud wail. "Mother! The painting is gone. Someone stole the painting out of the dollhouse!"

Mrs. Human came downstairs looking not at all concerned. She had been sewing, and she carried the sewing with her, working at it as she walked. "Peter, dear, quiet down," she said, ending her thread in a little knot and biting it off.

"How can you be so *calm* about it?" Peter cried. "It's a disaster!"

Mrs. Human put her arm around Peter, holding her sewing carefully so the pins would not prick him and said, "Let's just wait until the others come home. Maybe they know where it is."

"They don't CARE about my painting," Peter said. "Oh darn." He sat down on top of the sofa cushion on the floor.

And when the others came home, it was Harry of course who found the painting. He just looked about at the shambles Peter had made, and said, "It must have fallen down behind something." Then he moved the dollhouse, spilling everything over on its side, and exposed the Great Gap, which was wonderful indeed with all its dust puffles, reached in among them and took out the tiny painting wrapped so carefully in the patchwork quilt.

"Let me clean there," Mrs. Human said, gasping at the amount of whatever it was in the gap.

But Harry just said, "Is this it?" and pushed the trunk and the dollhouse back against the wall, hiding all the dirt once more.

Peter took the little package and unwrapped it. Silently. Silently he put the patchwork quilt back on the bed in the master bedroom. Silently he scruffled up the bit of yarn used to tie it with and stuffed it in his pocket.

"Really, Harry," he said at last.

Harry stared at Peter.

"Wrapping up the painting and hiding it like that."

"I didn't," Harry said. He looked as if he had been slapped.

"You expect me to believe that?"

"Yes," Harry said, "because it's true."

"Harry," Peter said, getting very red in the face because losing his temper was unusual for him, "you have ALWAYS done peculiar things to the dollhouse, even when you were little. I am not going to believe you." And he hung the picture back again over the mantelpiece where Mr. Dollhouse could contemplate it.

Harry went off to his room and cried because he was always being blamed for things, and Mrs. Human made Peter apologize, which he did but in a way that made it clear to Harry he didn't really mean it, and Kevin came home later and said they were both dumbbells because everyone was too big for the dollhouse anyway.

The Faces Return

It was while the Dollhouses were sitting around being depressed about Peter that the faces appeared again at the window. This time the lights were turned on in the dollhouse, so the family could not see outside very well. Mrs. Dollhouse was just saying, as she sewed up a tear in Baby's nightgown, "We'll just have to do POSITIVE thinking and decide that those awful men won't come here again," when the cat, standing on the table, froze, his ears perked forward, his broken nose in the air, his paw up. He was pointed toward the window.

Then the family heard something moving about outside in the darkness, and the voices of two men.

"Lucky they left those dollhouse lights on," one voice whispered. "Lets me see into the rooms without that lousy flashlight."

"Those little people," the younger voice said, "I saw 'em move!"

"You gettin' the spooks? You wanta be in on the job or not?" the older voice said.

"Sure, sure I wanta be in on it."

"Then don't imagine things. Them's dolls, dope." He paused for a moment. "The little lights make the whole little house look real, see, with the light coming out of the windows. But it's not real. You didn't see any of them dolls move, understand? Because that's a lot of baloney and I can't have baloney-type helpers with me."

"Okay, okay," the other voice said. "Forget it. Let's plan."

"Take the flash and go around the rest of the house—you know, case it. We got time if we're quiet and careful. Not like the other time when we had to beat it. I'll stay here, in the dark—pretty smart of us to smash that street light, wasn't it—I can see what I need from the dollhouse lights."

The younger man went off, and the older one peered around the dollhouse, talking softly to himself. "TV. Record set. Gold clock on the mantel. Gotta be careful not to break it . . ."

The younger robber returned. "Lots of silver in the dining room," he said. "Nice pictures in the living room. They keep a station wagon on the other side. It's locked, though."

"Got ski racks on it?"

"Yeah. Why?"

"That means they're going skiing. Probably over a weekend. What luck. We just keep a watch and when they all drive away, *zoom,* in we come and take whatever we want—fast— 'cause we know the layout. We can even do it in the daytime!"

"You're smart, George," the younger face said. "You figure they'll go skiing after Christmas? Then we can get all the presents, too."

"You're not so dumb either," George said

admiringly. "Take a last look in here. You know where the stuff is, it's easy later."

"Those toys there, on the funny bookcase," the younger voice said. "They're all old-fashioned. And that train—I ain't ever seen a train like that."

"Nice work," George said. "Those old toys are a Big Deal nowadays. Easy to sell. Antiques they're called."

A car rounded the top of the hill, its head-lights shining upward into the treetops. The shadow where the men stood was deep and black. The car shifted gears, then drove off.

"Let's blow," George said, "till the skiing time."

And the Dollhouses could hear the footsteps running off, and then, again, the sound of a car starting up and driving into the distance.

"Mother!" Ruth yelled, "are *we* antiques?" She ran to Mrs. Dollhouse and buried her head in her mother's lap, which was hard to do because Mrs. Dollhouse's lap was already full of Baby and torn nightgown.

"Boy," Todd said, "it's just like the end of the world, it's so scary." But his words were only show-off words, and he moved close to his father and took his hand.

Mr. Dollhouse smoothed Todd's head, coughed, and said at last, "The time has come to warn Kevin."

Everyone groaned.

"Listen to me," Mr. Dollhouse said. "Every other warning has fallen, as the saying goes, on deaf ears. Harry feels persecuted, Peter just got mad. But Kevin is the eldest—and the wisest—"

Everyone groaned again.

"Even if he's not so lovable anymore," Mr. Dollhouse added. "But I have an idea. Now perk up, all of you, and listen to me."

So they all perked up and listened.

"Kevin has hidden those terrible bomb things in the secret place. No one, not even Harry, knows about the secret place."

"So?" Mrs. Dollhouse asked.

"So, every now and again, Kevin checks on the bombs, right? Supposing he found something in *with* the bombs, something we put there, a very special thing. He'd think twice, maybe even three times about it. Wondering. He might even discover the broken window . . . It's a desperate try, but . . ." He paused and turned toward Mrs. Dollhouse. "I'm sorry, my dear, that you cleaned up the blood spot. It would have been a nice, frightening clue."

"It'll never work," Ruth said. "They're hopeless about getting messages."

"What could we put there?" Mrs. Dollhouse asked.

"My arm!" Todd said. "Boy, would that surprise him!"

Mr. Dollhouse smiled fondly at Todd. "I

wish you were right, Todd. But you lose your arms so often, he might not think much of it—except that the arm was in his secret place. No, it has to be something more fundamental than that—

"It has to be my head!"

They all gasped.

Into the silence Mr. Dollhouse spoke again. "No arguments, please. This is my own decision. I will need a little help, though. Come on now, Todd," he said, prodding his speechless son, "you'll have to help pull my head off and put it under the stairs. Peter stuffed me into the toilet again last night, so you'll have to put the rest of me in the toilet, leaving the head under the stairs. Let's see now how we can work it—"

"If you'll just get yourself up to the bathroom, I suppose I can do it," Todd said. "Boy," he added, "I sure hope Kevin doesn't stick your head in his pocket when he finds it!"

"Oh heavens," Mrs. Dollhouse said, "suppose he *never* finds it!"

"Be brave, Mother," Ruth said. "We can

manage to get Father's head out *somehow* every night."

"Not if Kevin absentmindedly leaves it in his own room," Mrs. Dollhouse said. She was having a hard time holding back her tears.

Todd patted his mother on the shoulder. "Just pray Kevin doesn't use Father's head when he plays marbles."

"Todd, sometimes I think you ought to be pushed overboard," Ruth said.

"I'm sorry," Todd said. "I didn't mean to make you cry. Kevin hardly ever plays marbles."

"Well," said Mr. Dollhouse, "it's getting early. Let's to work." He led the whole family up to the bathroom, where he sat down on the toilet so he would be a more convenient height for everyone. He said, "Farewell for a little, my dear," to Mrs. Dollhouse, "Take care of your mother," to Ruth, kissed the baby, and said, "Behave yourself," to Todd. Then he offered his head.

Mrs. Dollhouse and Todd pulled it off carefully. Then they turned the rest of Mr. Doll-

house around and stuffed him into the toilet before they carried his head downstairs, carefully removed the little panel, and tucked the head in next to the terrifying bombs.

It was very lonely with Mr. Dollhouse tucked away like that, so they all went off to bed way before dawn.

Kevin Looks Around

As it turned out, that was the very night Kevin chose to check on his firecrackers. Early, early, before the sun was up very far, he came downstairs and knelt in front of the dollhouse.

"Got to see if they're safe," he explained, half to himself and half to the dollhouse. "Want to shoot them off on New Year's Eve after we're back from skiing. Yes, sir. There they are."

His huge hand felt around in the secret place, checking the cherry bombs—and then Kevin felt something else. "What the—?" He pulled out Mr. Dollhouse's head. "Now how?" He sat back on his heels and stared in disbelief at the head. Then he checked the rest of Mr. Dollhouse, in the toilet. Sure enough, he was headless. Then Kevin looked at everything. He found the broken window in no time at all, and put his hand through it, wonderingly.

He stooped down and looked through the broken window—right out and up to the broken street light.

"Weird," Kevin said. And he popped Mr. Dollhouse's head into his bathrobe pocket. "I'll just wait," he said, "and see if that busybody Harry or that nutty Peter knows about my bombs."

And back he went to bed, not sure, somehow, that he was doing the right thing, but doing it anyway.

That whole week before Christmas the dollhouse family was miserable. Worst of all was the process each evening of taking Mr. Dollhouse out of the toilet and propping him against the bathtub. Finally Todd said, "Really, Mother, can't we prop him in the hall? He's so depressing when I'm taking a bath." And after that they carried him out of the bathroom every night and put him into the hall.

The human family was busy and happy that week before Christmas. The boys made presents all over the house, losing every tool their father owned in the process. They wrapped things up messily and noisily, they brought in a huge tree and decorated it, they were full of secrets from each other, and, as their mother and father noticed, were very very helpful and cooperative. "It's the best week in the year," Mrs. Human said, fondly watching Kevin as he bustled about, chopping wood for the fireplace. The boys even did as they were told, and organized their ski clothes—a job that caused them to climb the stairs to the attic some fifteen times, yelling questions continually. "Where is my headband, Mom?" "Did anyone see my long underwear, the pair with no holes in it?" "My boots are too small," a loud wail from Harry informed everyone. "Everything fits in but my toes." They helped their father scrape and wax the skis. They oiled the bindings—

and all that out of the way, set to once again, finishing up their endless wrapping and secrets and shopping.

And all of them forgot all about the doll-house.

Until Christmas Eve. It snowed on Christmas Eve. The sky, during this time of year when the days were short anyway, darkened at midafternoon. The lanterns stood in the hallway, ready to be lighted and carried tonight as everyone went caroling from house to house.

"It's the magic time," Harry said. He solemnly opened the front door and put an enormous candle on the front stoop. His mother lighted it for him and stood still long enough to admire it in the darkling twilight.

Then Harry went to the kitchen and reappeared carrying a large plate filled with sugar.

Kevin watched his youngest brother, his head cocked to one side. "What's that for?"

"The reindeer," Harry said. "I heard about it from a kid at school." He placed the plate of sugar next to the candle. "This kid said he

always did it and every year the sugar is licked away by morning. Really."

Peter lunged suddenly down the stairs from the second floor. "For heaven's sake," he said, "the floor's all covered with grunchy sugar. Harry, you slob, what are you doing?"

Kevin turned around from watching Harry out in the snow with the plate. "It's for the reindeer," he explained solemnly to Peter.

"Oh," Peter said. He scratched his head for a moment and said nothing more.

Harry, finished with the front stoop, entered the playroom with his brothers. Without a word, Harry knelt down and began arranging the dollhouse. Peter switched on the lights, and, together, the two brothers made order out of chaos. They straightened the pictures and lined up the furniture, and then Peter said, over his shoulder, to Kevin, "We almost forgot them this year. You making them a tree?"

Kevin did not reply. He was watching Peter take Mr. Dollhouse out of the toilet. Peter pulled up the headless body, then took the toilet and turned it upside down and shook it. "Now *where* in the world?" Peter said to himself, and proceeded to make a shambles of the house as he looked for Mr. Dollhouse's missing head.

Kevin just stood and watched. Harry joined the search. Finally, he and Peter simply tipped the house and dumped everything out on the floor of the playroom. No head. They put everything back again, neatly, talking to each other about the head.

"Maybe it's down *behind*," Harry said.

"You wouldn't have put it there by any chance?" Peter asked.

Harry punched him in the ribs.

It was Kevin who reminded them that it was

Christmas Eve, and they were both so surprised at him that they forgot their argument and did not, of course, find Mr. Dollhouse's head.

"You making a tree for them?" Peter asked Kevin again.

"I'm too busy," Kevin said, and went off to his room where he carefully took Mr. Dollhouse's head out of his bathrobe pocket, waited until his brothers had gone into the kitchen, sneaked downstairs, and then said loudly from the playroom, "I found it! I found the head!" and put it on Mr. Dollhouse firmly and then sat Mr. Dollhouse down in the parlor.

"Where'dja find it?" Harry called.

"Around," Kevin called back.

Harry looked at Peter and shrugged.

"I *looked* around," Peter said softly.

"Well, let's be glad it's back," Harry replied.

"Moving Specialists"

The Dollhouses were overjoyed that Mr. Dollhouse was himself again. Todd wanted to know what it was like in the pocket and Mr. Dollhouse said, "Grungy." But his remark, which made Todd and Ruth laugh, hid his deep worry about the robbers.

After all, nothing had worked. And when Mr. Human went off skiing, he, Mr. Dollhouse, would be the only adult male around. The responsibility was very very heavy.

Christmas Day came and went—or, in any event, happened. In the human family, Christmas Day was like a huge, friendly cyclone that struck giving only pleasure, and finally went away in the evening leaving everyone exhausted. Harry got new ski boots which he wore about the house "breaking them in," and leaving marks on the floors and saying "AOK" and giving directions to imaginary assistants because the boots made him feel like a moonwalker. Peter got acrylic paints in tubes, and spent a lot of the day painting a mural on his wall of a man lying under a tree with a hat

over his face, flowers blooming all around him and birds flapping about, singing. He made the music notes purple. Kevin got a typewriter and a leather sombrero and sat in the playroom the entire day writing a novel, wearing his pajamas and the hat. Mr. Human took pictures of all this chaos, and Mrs. Human picked things up.

That night Mrs. Dollhouse, who was sitting on the sofa with Mr. Dollhouse, resting her head against his neck and being happy that he was all attached together again, said, "They can't possibly go skiing. The whole human house is a mess and they're all too tired. Anyway, the boys won't want to leave their Christmas."

She was wrong. The humans left their house in a mess "so it'll still be Christmas when we come home," as Harry cheerily put it, packed themselves into the car, and went off down the snowy hill to find even snowier hills on which to ski.

Mr. Dollhouse sat and wondered what to do. Most of the day he sat, telling the children to run off and not bother him every time they came into the living room. And they came into the living room many times because it was so rare for them to have a whole day of complete freedom from the humans.

"Father, come and see what we're doing!" Todd shouted. "We're making a tower of the blocks in the nursery and we're going to knock it down!"

"I'm THINKING," Mr. Dollhouse said, and the children scampered off. As he sat and thought, he could hear them upstairs, laughing and arguing and talking. Then he heard Todd's clear voice saying, "Okay, Baby, pull out the bottom block!" and boom, crash, the block tower came tumbling down. It sounded like a thunderclap.

And the idea came to Mr. Dollhouse like a thunderclap too.

He almost ran from the living room to the stairs, pried open the panel, and crawled inside with the cherry bombs.

Very carefully and slowly, he pushed the bombs, one at a time, into the living room and placed them next to the sofa, and stood back. "Out of the way," he said to himself, "but conveniently located in case of emergency."

Struggling, because they were as thick as ropes to him, he twisted the three fuses together. Then he placed the small plastic chest of drawers over the bombs, and it fitted perfectly, looking like an end table. Since it was really a fake chest, having no back or bottom at all, it slipped into place easily.

Where he was going to go from there Mr. Dollhouse was not sure; everything depended on the robbers. But he felt so much better about the whole situation that he ran upstairs like a boy and built the children a block tower that went almost to the ceiling of the nursery.

In the afternoon, Mrs. Dollhouse decided

the children were exhausting themselves, being up all day, and persuaded them to take naps—after all, they had a whole night to go through. As a special concession, because Todd and Ruth felt it was humiliating to take naps, they were allowed to sleep on the hallway floor on top of their patchwork quilts. Mr. and Mrs. Dollhouse stretched out together on the sofa.

The robbers arrived at nap time. In a green truck, which they parked boldly in the driveway. Calmly, they separated, and went to the front door and the back door of the humans' house. The older robber, at the back door, made small, pinging, scritchy noises as he tried to open the lock.

The Dollhouses woke up all at once. Mr. Dollhouse sprang off the sofa and stood, listening, in the parlor. Mrs. Dollhouse sat up, looking confused. Todd went to the window, where he could see out to the driveway. Ruth clutched her quilt about her, and Baby sucked his thumb. The cat crouched in the corner, bristling.

And sure enough, they heard the back-door

lock snap, and then the door opening—it always scraped a little when it opened. Then the older robber walked through the house, crouching a little and looking about, and opened the front door for the younger robber, who was dressed for the occasion in coveralls that said, "Moving Specialists" across the back.

And moving specialists they were. In no time at all, they unhitched the television set and carried it into the front hallway, ready to go into the truck. The older robber sneaked into the dining room and came back again through the playroom with a whole armload of shining silver: pitchers and candlesticks, platters and creamers. He dumped them, with a horrid clatter, next to the television set, turned around and came back this time with knives and forks and spoons sticking out of all his pockets, carrying a huge silver punch bowl. "Where's the sack?" he called, and the younger robber came into the hallway carrying the electric typewriter from the den.

"Got it in my back pocket," he said, turning around so George could get it out.

"Careful with that," George said. "Can't sell it if it's broke."

The younger robber set the typewriter down gently. Then he turned toward the playroom and saw Kevin's new typewriter in its case standing under the Christmas tree.

"What luck!" he said. "A brand-new one!" And he picked up the typewriter and stood still, looking over the collection of Christmas presents. "You want hockey skates, perfume, records, an easel, shirts, sweaters, books, puzzles and"— he stooped down and opened a very small box—"a pair of earrings?"

"Put it all in the sack," George said. "Not the easel and books, though. And get a move on. There's hi-fi junk in the living room."

The Dollhouses sat or stood exactly where they had frozen when the robbers arrived. Mr. Dollhouse, standing in the living room, felt completely helpless. I should have remembered, he thought, that when humans are around, I can't do *anything*. And such humans. If the place was a mess before, it looks now as if it had been attacked. And I can't move.

Putting It All Together

Riding along the snowy roads, the skis rattling comfortably on the roof of the station wagon, the human family drove swiftly northward. Mr. Human was singing, and Mrs. Human was harmonizing in the front seat. The three boys sat in their favorite place—the very back of the wagon, in the three small seats that formed a cozy nook, and from which they could look out through the back window, over the tailgate.

They were playing rummy on the floor, and the playing cards kept slipping about. Kevin, picking up the cards, counted them and said, "One's missing. Must have slipped under something on that last curve."

"Maybe you'll find it—*around*—" Peter said, and he and Harry nudged each other and giggled.

"What's the smirking about?" Kevin demanded.

"Like the dollhouse father's head, he means," Harry said. "We turned the room upside down looking and then you said you'd found the head 'around.' "

"You didn't believe me, huh?" Kevin asked. "I suppose you think I hid it in my room or something."

Harry and Peter just looked at him.

Kevin found the missing card and attended to the game. "As a matter of fact," he said, "I did."

"Did you put the picture down behind the trunk too?" Harry asked.

"Heck, no. You did."

"No, I didn't," Harry said. "If you really want to know."

"We don't necessarily want to know," Peter said.

"Oh, shut up, Peter," Kevin said. "You're probably the one who broke the window."

"What window?"

"The kitchen one," Harry explained. "I found it all broken and I swept up the pieces because I figured you guys would blame me."

They stared at him, holding their cards.

"Something's *up!*" Peter said.

Kevin held up his hand. "Now wait a minute. The window was broken, the painting was all wrapped up funny and stuffed into the crack, and the dollhouse man's head was—" he stopped himself. "In a strange place," he added softly.

"I looked through the broken window and I looked right out at the broken street light, the one that makes the yard so dark," Harry said, "while I was eating my—"

"Yes, sir," Peter interrupted him. "Something's up all right. I'm really sorry I blamed you, Harry."

"It's okay," Harry said. "This is serious," he added.

Kevin put all his cards into his right hand and made them into a neat little pile. He shook his head. "You mean to tell me that you two guys really think—"

"We really do," Peter said. "And you really do too, Kevin, and you know it."

"We have to go back," Harry said. "Those dollhouse people are trying to tell us something."

Kevin looked over his shoulder at his parents in the front of the car. Then he turned around again. "They'll never believe us," he said. "And anyway, Dad'll be so disappointed about skiing . . ."

"Not as disappointed as he'll be if he gets home in three days and finds the house robbed or something," Peter said.

"Yeah, but Kevin's right." Harry's voice was sad. "They'll never believe us."

"They'll also think we're crazy," Kevin pointed out. "Only reason they'd ever turn back is if one of us got sick." He paused. He and Peter looked expectantly at Harry.

Harry sighed. "Okay," he said at last. "I'll do it. But you guys have to promise to help. You know, like if Mom tries to make me stay in bed for two whole days or something, you gotta persuade her to let me out."

They promised.

Harry wound down the rear window of the station wagon, put his head out, put his finger into his throat—and threw up. Kevin held him and Peter informed his parents.

The singing stopped in the front seat, the

human father turned the car around, the human mother took Harry into the front seat with her, patted his forehead and said worriedly, "He's *very* hot," and they headed back home.

It was early afternoon.

The Bang-y Ending

To the dollhouse family, it looked as if George the robber and his helper had piled everything in the whole human house into the front hallway. Harry's precious rock collection had been brought down from upstairs—on a silver tray that the younger robber announced he'd found "in the big bedroom." Peter's guitar slung around his neck, George descended the staircase carrying Kevin's record player. From somewhere the robbers amassed a golf bag filled with Mr. Human's golf equipment, two good tennis rackets, a portable sewing machine, a leather box filled "with jools," as George explained, and a movie projector.

"We do it this way," George said, "all lined up. Then we just open the front door, go out and get the packing cartons from the truck, bring 'em in and put the loot in 'em—and carry them out again. Any neighbors watching, they think we're movers. But we do it quick."

The younger robber was standing in the playroom, looking all around. "Time for the antiques?"

"Yeah. Put them in the hallway so we can load 'em into the boxes. Just like perfessionals."

The younger robber smiled. "I feel REAL perfessional," he said, and he took a cigar out of his pocket and lighted it, sucking and blowing and sucking again. "Aah," he said as it glowed. Clamping the cigar between his teeth, he bent down and dismantled the old, large-size trains, uncoupling the steam engine from the coal car, then the passenger coaches one at a time, and carrying them into the hall. He went to the tall bookcase and removed the collection of old penny banks put there so lovingly over the years, marveling that they were so heavy.

On the bottom shelf was an iron truck, big enough for a little boy to ride on. It had high fenders and no windshield, and great skinny wheels painted red, with yellow spokes in them. He pushed the truck across the floor. "Look out, George! Here comes the Tin Lizzie!" and they both laughed as the truck bumped gently into the trains.

They removed the heavy mantel clock together and with care, and set it on the floor next to the truck.

Then, bold as anything, George opened the front door and went out to get the cartons. The younger robber took a look to see if he was really gone, then knelt down on the floor in front of the dollhouse. He studied everything, his smelly cigar reeking smoke into the little house. After a bit, he reached around and switched on the dollhouse lights. "Ain't that something," he said, and he looked at each room, at all the dollhouse family. He picked

up the baby from its crib, admired its beautiful bisque head, then gently replaced the baby in its bed.

George came back in the front door, his arms loaded with cartons. "What's the matter with you? Come get the rest of the cartons with me or I cut you out of the whole deal, understand? These people got neighbors. Neighbors with *eyes*. We can't take all day, dummy. And we *ain't* takin' the dollhouse, it's big and it'll spill. Now move!"

The younger robber moved, fast. He laid his cigar on the edge of the dollhouse living room, the lit end hanging over the edge, the wet,

chewed part right next to the sofa, and ran with George out of the front door to the drive-way to help with the cartons.

Instantly, Mr. Dollhouse ran across the living room to the sofa. "Todd!" he yelled. "Quick!"

Todd was quick. He helped his father move the fake chest of drawers. And his mouth dropped open at the sight of the bombs.

"Hurry! Push!" Together Mr. Dollhouse and Todd pushed and hauled. The weight of the bombs tied together was like that of a piano. Mr. Dollhouse's tuxedo ripped, and Todd's arm went backward in its loose socket. Somehow they managed to get the bombs around the sofa and around the wet cigar end, its stench almost choking them.

"Here, here, right at the edge," Mr. Doll-house ordered. Todd pushed. The bombs inched forward until they were right next to the cigar, and right on the very edge of the dollhouse.

Todd, out of breath, stood still. He could not believe what he was seeing. Mr. Dollhouse, cool as any of the television bomb men Todd had watched, bent the great ropes of the fuses and held them against the lighted end of the cigar.

Instantly the air was filled with a sickening, hissing noise. Huge sparks flew up from the twined fuses. Todd leaped back, covering his eyes. But his father's hand pulled him forward.

"Now, Todd, brave boy, now! with me, push. Push for your life, son!"

They pushed. The hissing deafened them, the sparks singed their arms, and the huge bombs rolled forward, backward, then—

"One big heave, Todd!"

The bombs went overboard.

George and his assistant opened the front door. Todd and his father froze in place.

"BOOOM!!!!!!!!"

That, Mr. Dollhouse thought as he sailed into the air and smashed against the ceiling of the dollhouse living room, was rather more than I had expected.

Everything loose in the playroom jumped and tumbled onto the floor. A big burned place appeared in the rug. The sound was more than sound. It could be heard in the stomach.

And it brought the humans' neighbors out in force. They appeared on the driveway, on the lawn.

George and his assistant made for the truck, started it up even as a man stuck his head in the cab window and said, "What's happening?"

"Outta da way!" George yelled, and he made off, wheels shrieking, almost knocking down three people as he went.

And, as the green truck went down the hill, the human family's station wagon came up the hill, slowed because of all the people, then pulled into the driveway.

Without a word, the whole family jumped out and ran to the house.

There was the door, open. Inside, the hall-

way was jammed with cartons and boxes and things.

And a terrible smell of gunpowder in the air.

Mr. Human and Mrs. Human sat down abruptly, heads in hands.

"Here," a neighbor's voice said. "I got the license number of the truck."

Mr. Human did not answer. Harry walked forward. "Thanks, Mr. Brown," he said. "They didn't take anything, I think. We were expecting something like this. It's why we came home."

And his mother and father raised their heads and looked at their youngest son as if he were a creature from Mars.

Peter went into the playroom. "You exaggerated, Harry. *I* sure didn't expect anything like *this!*"

Kevin looked at the shambles and at the scorch in the carpet. "Boy, me neither."

"Here's a clue," Harry said. He picked up the chewed and still lighted cigar from the living room of the dollhouse.

Kevin took the cigar and held it for a moment before he threw it into the fireplace.

"That's a *clue*," Harry said. "Don't throw it out."

"Okay, okay, Harry. But it stinks. The police will find the robbers from the license number. We don't *need* that icky old cigar. Forget it."

Harry stood and glared at his eldest brother. "Kevin," he said, "there is something you know that we don't."

Kevin reached over and ruffled Harry's hair. "You're so right," he said.

Later, hours later, after all the things in the hallway had been sorted out, after Harry had repaired his dollhouse piano, after Peter had made his mother sit down NOW and mend Mr. Dollhouse's tuxedo, after the policemen had come, walking importantly in their high leather boots and shaking their heads in wonder at the mess—and gone away—and then telephoned to say they had found the green truck and George and his assistant enjoying a flat tire on the Thruway, then the three boys heard their father say over the telephone:

"You mean *they* don't know what caused the explosion? Really? Well, I guess we'll never know."

Harry piped up, "I found a cig—" but Kevin's hand over his mouth stopped the words.

Quickly, before Harry could object, Kevin said, "Want to help me make the dollhouse a Christmas tree?" and Harry, thrilled, forgot what he had started to say and ran out into the snow to help Kevin cut a perfect sprig from the spruce tree.

As he hung a tiny set of glass beads on the tree, Harry said, "You said the dollhouse was babyish, Kev."

"Changed my mind."

Harry sighed happily.

Peter, busy doctoring up Mr. Dollhouse's battered head with his paints, looked over at his brothers. "Christmas was yesterday," he remarked.

"So I'm a little late," Kevin said. "So what?"

"So," Harry said, "there's still something you know that we don't."

Kevin sat back on his heels and watched as Peter put the dollhouse father on the sofa where he could see the painting—and the Christmas tree. "There's something I know that you don't," Kevin repeated. "But there's something you two have always known that I forgot. How's *that* for a conundrum, Harry?"

"How come you can make up conundrums?" Peter asked. "That's very cool."

Kevin turned red in the face. " 'S 'nothing," he said. "Just part of growing up." He picked up a bit of silver paper and cut it into a star shape. In tiny letters he printed, "For Bravery Under Fire" on it and then stuck it on Mr. Dollhouse's tuxedo front.

His brothers watched, wondering.

When nighttime came, Mr. Dollhouse, first thing, took off the star and stuck it on Todd.

"We'll just leave it there," he said, "they'll understand."

Todd stuck his chest out and strutted about the room. "Boy," he said, "just think. We did it. We saved the humans' house."

Mrs. Dollhouse looked out over the playroom. "In a manner of speaking," she added, and Mr. Dollhouse and the children laughed.

"And we're really responsible for putting those guys in the cooler," Todd said. "Imagine that."

"In the what?"

"The cooler," Todd said. "That's a jail."

"Don't tell me. I know you learned it on television," Mr. Dollhouse said.

And it was time for breakfast again.

Mrs. Dollhouse sang as she made the scrambled eggs in the huge pan, and sang as she tucked her pretty baby into his high chair, and sang as she smoothed Ruth's terrible hair, and sang as she fed the cat with the broken nose, and sang as she pushed Todd's arm back in its socket, and sang as she admired her handsome husband dressed in his tuxedo, because she knew now that the human boys would never never give the dollhouse away to anyone, and she knew that they wouldn't even put it on the shelf to Wait For The Next Generation.

And they never did.

THE END

For BRAVERY UNDER FIRE